CUENTO
DE LUZ

Grandpa Monty's Muddles

Text © 2012 Marta Zafrilla
Illustrations © 2012 Miguel Ángel Díez
This edition © 2012 Cuento de Luz SL
Calle Claveles 10 | Urb Monteclaro | Pozuelo de Alarcón | 28223 Madrid | Spain | www.cuentodeluz.com
Original title in Spanish: Los despistes del abuelo Pedro
English translation by Jon Brokenbrow
2nd printing
ISBN: 978-84-15241-17-1

Printed by Shanghai Chenxi Printing Co., Ltd. in PRC, february 2013, print number 1339

FSC
www.fsc.org
MIX
Paper from
responsible sources
FSC® C007923

Grandpa Monty's Muddles

Text
Marta Zafrilla

Illustrations
Miguel Ángel Díez

You might think that it's easy to start telling a story, but it isn't. It REALLY isn't. And I don't want to do that thing when you start by saying, "Hi everyone, I'm Oscar, I'm seven years old, and I'm an only child."
No way! I wanted to do something more original.

But I can't think of anything better, so all I'll say is:

Hi everyone, I'm Oscar, I'm seven years old, and I'm an only child.

See what I mean? You try to get straight to the point, say things just the way they are, and instead things get more complicated. My name is really Samuel Oscar, but everyone just calls me Oscar. And I'm not only seven years old: I'm seven years, two months and ten days old. And for the last three months, I haven't been an only child.

It's not because I've got a little brother who's crying and pooping all over the place, no sir. It's because Grandpa Monty has come to live with us.

I know, I know... a grandpa isn't like
a little brother, but you'll see what I
mean. My grandpa isn't very well, and a
lot of the things he says and does make
him look like a little kid.

But let's not get carried away; the best thing
to do is to start at...

The beginning.

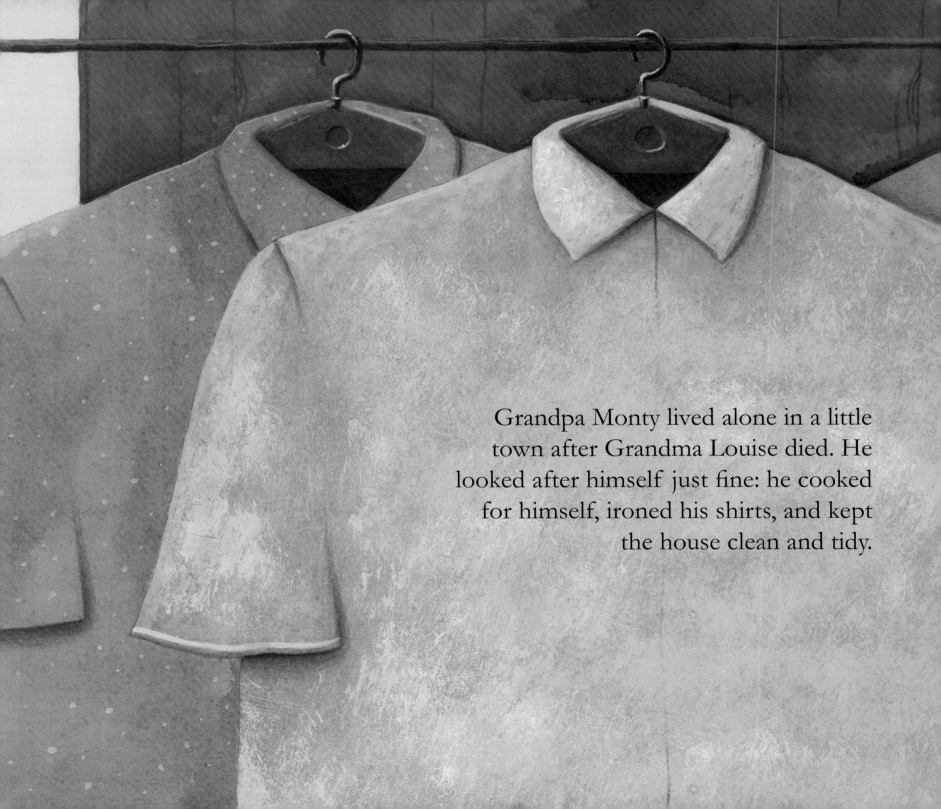

Grandpa Monty lived alone in a little town after Grandma Louise died. He looked after himself just fine: he cooked for himself, ironed his shirts, and kept the house clean and tidy.

But one day, Uncle Andrew found out that in just one week, Grandpa Monty had put a chicken in the washing machine, roasted a sweater, and ironed a piece of fish!

At first, Mom thought he was doing it to get our attention so we'd go and visit him more often, but when the police called us one day to tell us Grandpa was trying to open a tree with the keys to his mailbox, she got really worried.

Grandpa Monty wasn't well, and he needed our help.

Uncle Andrew was out all day, so Grandpa came to live with us because we could look after him and keep him company. Dad's office was turned into Grandpa's bedroom, and soon the smell of lavender and tartan blankets replaced Dad's shelves, books and files.

The fact is, our schedules work perfectly: when Mom and I are at school, Dad looks after Grandpa, and when Dad goes to work, we're already at home. So Grandpa is never alone. But, of course, we can't be looking out for him all of the time, and though we even leave the door open when we go to the bathroom, sometimes Grandpa Monty gets up to all sorts of things!

The worst thing about Grandpa's illness, as you'll realize, is that he mixes up towels with napkins, gloves with socks, and biscuits with medicines. If we all keep an eye on him, we can make sure he doesn't tread on Yoko (our cat) or try to turn on the TV with an eggplant (although sometimes that's funny).
What's really sad is that, little by little, he seems to forget which words to use.

At first I thought it was my fault, and that he was forgetting them so that I'd learn them. But Mom explained to me that it wasn't that; he was just forgetting them, and it had nothing to do with me.

Grandfather Monty and Grandmother Louise.

The doctor says that to exercise your memory, it's good to read the newspaper every day, look at old photo albums, and to do math where you add up and take away. Every afternoon, Grandpa helps me with my homework, and then I help him with his. So that way I learn, and he remembers.

Every afternoon we look at photos of when Mom was a little girl, photos of Grandpa Monty when he was young, of Uncle Andrew, Auntie Christine, cousins Jennifer, Peter, Irene, Oliver and Michael. He repeats the names belonging to all of the faces, and I've ended up memorizing them too.

37
− 15

1968
+ 37

To stop Grandpa Monty from getting in a muddle, one day when Mom went to the doctor, I covered the house with notes with the names of things. I began with all of the things that started with "S": sweater, stool, sink, salt shaker, sandals... and then all of the words that started with "C": couch, car, cracker, cookies...

And then the ones that start with "M":
melon, mousetrap, mantelpiece, milk…
The last letter I used to write on the notes was "Y"
for Yoko and yell. The cat wasn't too happy
about having her name taped to her tail,
and when Mom saw Yoko jumping around and the house
full of notes with thumbtacks and tape…she yelled.

She yelled a lot.

Fortunately, Dad let me off easy, saying that although making holes all over the house wasn't the best idea in the world, I'd been trying to help Grandpa Monty.

But I wasn't allowed to watch TV and I had
to pick up all of the notes I'd stuck all over
the house, I kept the thumbtacks and tape
and I put the notes with the words on them
in an empty photo album. The next day,
I gave Grandpa his first "word album,"
which was really a miniature dictionary
with the words from around our house.

Unfortunately Grandpa Monty isn't getting any better. Every day he remembers fewer names and fewer things. Yesterday he didn't recognize me; instead of calling me Oscar, he began to call me Pumpkin. Even though my head isn't that big! But every afternoon we keep doing our homework.

This week I'm making him an album with the names of the states and their capital cities. Now I can go over what I learn at school, and Grandpa can exercise his memory.

Do you make albums with everything you learn, too?

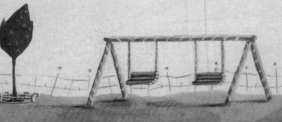

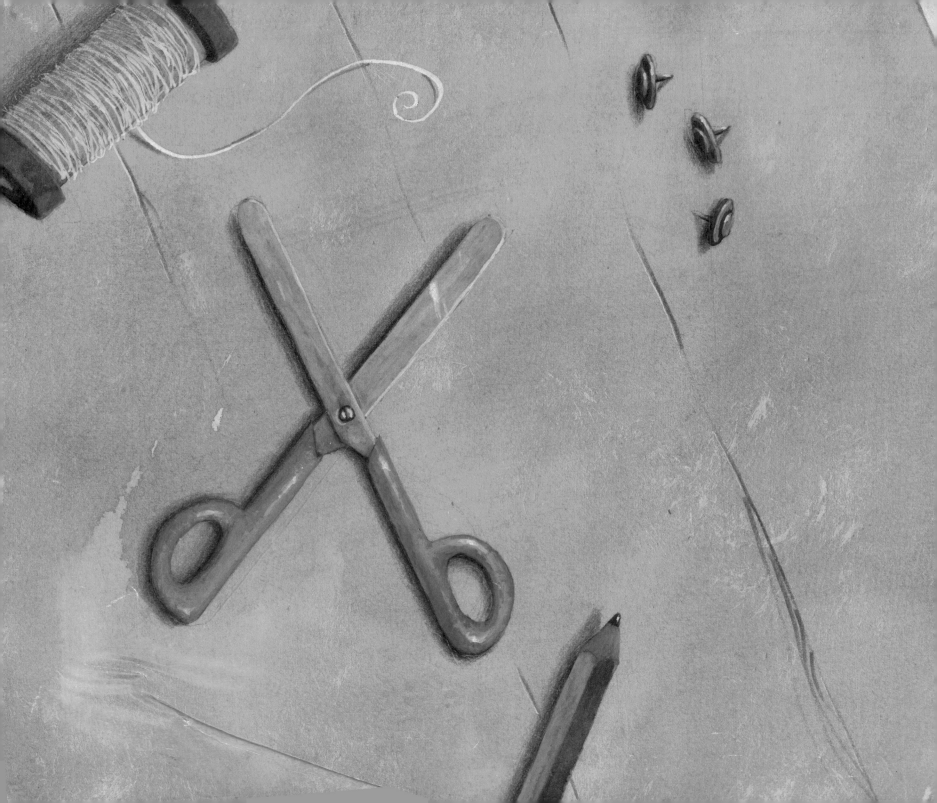

SIMON BOOM
Gives a Wedding

by YURI SUHL ✑ illustrated by MARGOT ZEMACH

FOUR WINDS PRESS / NEW YORK

SECOND PRINTING 1973
FIRST PRINTING 1972
PUBLISHED BY FOUR WINDS PRESS
A DIVISION OF SCHOLASTIC MAGAZINES, INC., NEW YORK, N.Y.
TEXT COPYRIGHT © 1972 YURI SUHL
ILLUSTRATIONS COPYRIGHT © 1972 MARGOT ZEMACH
ALL RIGHTS RESERVED.
PRINTED IN THE UNITED STATES OF AMERICA
LIBRARY OF CONGRESS CATALOGUE CARD NUMBER: 70-161015

Once there was a man named Simon Boom who liked to boast: "I buy only the best." It didn't matter if the best was a size too short, or a size too long, or altogether out of season. If it was the best, Simon Boom bought it.

One summer day Simon Boom walked into a hat store and said to the storekeeper: "Give me the best hat you have."

"Very well," said the storekeeper and brought out the best straw hat in the store.

"Is this the best you have?" said Simon Boom.

"In straw hats, yes," the storekeeper replied.

"I mean the best of *all* hats," Simon Boom said.

"I have a still better hat," said the storekeeper, "but it's made of felt."

"I don't want a better hat," Simon Boom said. "I want the best hat."

"Very well," said the storekeeper. "The very best hat I have is made of lamb's wool. It will keep your head warm on the coldest day."

"If it is the very best I'll buy it," said Simon Boom. And he did.

That summer all the men in town felt comfortable in their light hats. Only Simon Boom was perspiring in his heavy winter hat.

"My head feels so warm," thought Simon Boom, "I'll buy myself an umbrella to protect it from the sun." And so he walked into an umbrella store and said to the storekeeper: "Give me the best umbrella you have."

"Beach umbrella, or rain umbrella?" the storekeeper asked.

"Best umbrella," said Simon Boom.

"Very well," said the storekeeper. He pulled a black umbrella out of the umbrella stand and snapped it open. "This is the best I have," he said. "Strong fabric, sturdy frame, steel ribs. Guaranteed to protect you from the rain."

"If it's the best I'll buy it," said Simon Boom. And he did.

Now Simon Boom was the only person in town wearing a winter hat and carrying an open rain umbrella on a bright summer day.

The umbrella didn't help much and Simon Boom thought, "I'll buy myself a light suit to keep cool." And so he walked into a clothing store and said to the salesman: "Give me the best suit you have."

"Seersucker or gabardine?" the salesman asked.

"The best," Simon Boom replied.

"The best of each?" the salesman wanted to know.

"The best in the store," Simon Boom told him.

"Very well," said the salesman and brought out an Irish tweed suit. "This is made of the finest wool. Guaranteed to keep you warm on the coldest day. But it may be a little too large for you. What size do you wear?"

"I wear a thirty-eight short," said Simon Boom.

"This suit is forty-two long," said the salesman, "and it's the only one left. I'm sorry."

"If it's the best I'll buy it," Simon Boom said. And he did.

Now Simon Boom was the only person in town wearing a warm winter hat, a warm winter suit, and carrying an open umbrella on a bright summer day.

Simon Boom had an only daughter, named Rosalie. When the time came for Rosalie to get married Simon Boom said to his wife: "I am going to give the best wedding party ever held in this town. I'll invite the best people and serve the best food. It will be a wedding party the whole town will talk about. I want nothing but the best for my daughter."

"What shall we serve our guests," his wife asked, "fish or fowl?"

"Fish," said Simon Boom. "All kinds of fish. Bluefish, whitefish, swordfish, flounder, tuna, halibut, cod, salmon, mackerel and lots more."

Three days before the wedding Simon Boom went to see the fish dealer. "I will need two hundred pounds of the very best fish for my daughter's wedding," he said to the man, who wore a brown leather cap and an apron that smelled of fish. "All kinds of fish."

"Very well," said the fish dealer. "You shall have all the fish you want."

"But I want the *best* fish," Simon Boom said.

"Our fish are as sweet as sugar," said the fish dealer.

"Did you say sweet as sugar?" Simon Boom asked.

"Upon my word, sir," the fish dealer said. "Sweet as sugar."

"Aha," thought Simon Boom to himself. "If he said sweet as sugar, then sugar must be better than fish. I shall get sugar instead." And so he said to the fish dealer, "I have changed my mind," and left.

Simon Boom went straight to the sugar merchant and said, "I will need two hundred pounds of sugar for my daughter's wedding."

"Very well, sir," said the sugar merchant, whose face and eyebrows, and cap, and apron were all covered with sugar powder. "You shall have all the sugar you want."

"But I want the very best sugar," Simon Boom told the man.

"Our sugar is as sweet as honey," said the sugar merchant.

"Did you say sweet as honey?" Simon Boom asked.

"Upon my word, sir," the sugar merchant said. "Sweet as honey."

"Aha," Simon Boom thought to himself. "If he said sweet as honey then honey must be better than sugar. I shall get honey instead." And so he said to the sugar merchant, "I have changed my mind," and left.

Simon Boom went straight to the honey merchant and said, "I want two hundred jars of honey for my daughter's wedding."

"Very well," said the honey merchant, who wore a white cap and a white coat and smelled of honey. "You shall have all the honey you want."

"But I want the very best honey you have," Simon Boom said.

"Our honey is as clear as oil," said the honey merchant.

"Did you say clear as oil?" Simon Boom asked.

"Upon my word, sir," said the honey merchant. "Clear as oil."

"Aha," Simon Boom thought to himself. "If he said clear as oil then oil must be better than honey. I shall get oil instead." And so he said to the honey merchant, "I have changed my mind," and he left.

Simon Boom then went straight to the oil merchant and said, "I want two hundred quarts of oil for my daughter's wedding."

"Very well, sir," said the oil merchant, who wore a dark leather coat and a dark leather cap that smelled of oil. "You shall have all the oil you want."

"But I want the very best oil," Simon Boom said.

"Our oil is as pure as spring water," said the oil merchant.

"Did you say pure as spring water?" Simon Boom asked.

"Upon my word, sir," the oil merchant said, "as pure as spring water."

"Aha," Simon Boom thought to himself. "If he said as pure as spring water then spring water must be better than oil. I shall get spring water instead." And so he said to the oil merchant, "I have changed my mind," and he left.

Simon Boom wandered all over town looking for a spring water store and couldn't find one. He was about to give up when he saw the water carrier with two wooden cans of water hanging from the yoke on his shoulders. "Maybe he would know," Simon Boom thought to himself. "He deals in water." And so he ran up to the water carrier and said, "Pardon me, could you please tell me where I can buy some spring water?"

"I certainly can," said the water carrier, setting down his two cans on the ground, for they were very heavy.

"At last!" said Simon Boom, feeling much happier now. "I have been looking for that spring water store all over town and couldn't find it."

"No wonder!" said the water carrier. "The water you are looking for is not in a store. It's in a well."

"But I want spring water," said Simon Boom, "not well water."

"My dear sir," said the water carrier, "well water is the purest, coolest spring water there is."

"Is it also the best?" Simon Boom asked.

"The very best," said the water carrier.

"If it is the very best," said Simon Boom, "then I want twenty barrelsful for my daughter's wedding."

"You shall have all the well water you want," said the water carrier. "When is the wedding?"

"In three days," said Simon Boom.

"I'll deliver it just before the guests arrive so the water will be fresh and cool," the water carrier told Simon Boom.

When Simon Boom came home his wife said, "You look happy. That means you got the fish you wanted."

"Not fish and not sugar either," said Simon Boom.

"You bought chicken instead?"

"Not chicken and not honey either," said Simon Boom.

"You bought beef instead?"

"Not beef and not oil either," Simon Boom said.

"Then what *did* you buy?" his wife wanted to know.

"I bought something that is sweeter than sugar, clearer than honey, purer than oil, and better than all three of them."

"Doesn't it have a name?" his wife asked.

"It has," said Simon Boom. "The Best."

"The best what?"

"That, my dear wife, I want to be a surprise even to you," said Simon Boom.

"But will it come in time for me to cook it?" his wife asked.

"It doesn't have to be cooked," Simon Boom said.

"It doesn't have to be cooked? My, that *is* a surprise."

"It's the Best," said Simon Boom, smiling happily.

A few hours before the wedding party was to begin Mrs. Boom ordered the servants to set the table. When Simon Boom walked into the dining room and saw what they were doing he shouted to the servants: "Off with the plates! Off with the knives! Off with the forks! Off with the spoons! Only the glasses remain!"

Just then Simon Boom's wife walked into the dining room. When she saw what was happening she was very confused. "I ordered the table set," she reminded the servants.

"And I ordered it unset," Simon Boom told her. "For my special dish all we need is glasses."

"Not even plates, and knives, and forks, and spoons?" his wife said. "That *is* a surprise!"

"The Best," said Simon Boom, smiling happily again.

The water carrier kept his promise. Shortly before the guests began to arrive he rolled the twenty barrelsful of well water up the hill to Simon Boom's house. As soon as the wedding ceremony was over Simon Boom ordered the servants to fill every pitcher in the house with water from the barrels and place them all around the table.

It was a warm evening and as soon as the guests arrived they filled their glasses and drank. "Ah," they said, "fresh, cold water! That's just what we need."

"See how they love it?" said Simon Boom to his wife. "That's because we are serving the Best, the *very* Best." And he ordered the servants to keep the pitchers full.

Soon the musicians struck up a jolly wedding tune and the guests began to dance. When the dance was over the guests were warm and thirsty.

They went back to the table for some fresh, cold water. Simon Boom watched them fill up their glasses and he said to his wife: "You see what happens when you serve the Best? They love it."

Now the guests were beginning to get hungry and they were waiting for food. But all they got was more water. They filled their glasses and drank it. "Look how they drink it," said Simon Boom to his wife. "They just don't seem to get enough of that wonderful well water."

The musicians struck up another lively tune, but the guests were now too hungry to get up and dance. So they remained seated at the table, and to keep their stomachs from rumbling they drank some more water. "Our guests must be pretty hungry by now," said Mrs. Boom to her husband. "All we have been giving them is water. Don't you think we should give them something to eat too?"

"Absolutely not!" said Simon Boom. "We are serving the Best, and there is nothing better than the Best."

By midnight the guests were so full of water that they couldn't even keep their eyes open, and they all fell asleep at the table.

"Maybe if they had some food they might be able to stay awake," said Mrs. Boom.

"What they need is some more of that fresh, cold water to wake them up," said Simon Boom, and he ordered the servants to fill up all the glasses.

"Sorry," said the servants, "but the pitchers are empty."

"Then fill up the pitchers!" Simon Boom commanded.

"Sorry," said the servants, "but the barrels, too, are empty."

"Then fill up the barrels!" Simon Boom ordered the servants. "Roll them down to the well and fill them up. Hurry! Hurry! Hurry!" he shouted.

The guests were awakened by Simon Boom's shouting and they thought that, at last, the food was about to be served. "I wish to make an announcement," Simon Boom said. "I know that you would all like to have some more of that fresh, cool well water. So please be patient. I just sent my servants to the well. They will soon return with twenty barrelsful of the same water. The Best."

When the guests heard that more water was coming they groaned. They all got up and made for the door. In a few minutes they were all gone.

"Now look what you have done!" Mrs. Boom said to her husband, and she burst into tears. "I'll never live down the shame," she muttered, as she dabbed her eyes with her handkerchief. "Won't you *ever* listen to me? Imagine, serving only water at my daughter's wedding party!"

"Only water!" Simon Boom shouted. "But what *kind* of water? I served them water that is:

> sweeter than sugar,
>
> clearer than honey,
>
> purer than oil,
>
> and better than all three of them.
>
> I served them the Best.
>
> The *very* Best!"